Ross Hunter has always loved teaching, travel and writing. His four decades 'at the chalkface' and in the Head's office, have taken Sue and him around UK, Europe, Russia and Asia. After many dozens of magazine articles, *A Maltese Crossing* is his first novel. He is an avid collector of maps, books, and travel clutter. His ideal year would be spent in Lancashire, France, Moscow and SE Asia, on a bicycle when possible, and not flying. He speaks English, (ef)fluent French and some Russian, plus a few bits and pieces. Lockdown has meant virtual travel, so more writing.

Dedicated with lifelong thanks and love to Sue,
and to our families.

Ross Hunter

A MALTESE CROSSING

AUSTIN MACAULEY PUBLISHERS™

LONDON • CAMBRIDGE • NEW YORK • SHARJAH

A CIP catalogue record for this title is available from the British Library.

ISBN 9781398435032 (Paperback)
ISBN 9781398435049 (ePub e-book)

www.austinmacauley.com

First Published 2022
Austin Macauley Publishers Ltd®
1 Canada Square
Canary Wharf
London
E14 5AA

Grateful thanks to Lorraine Atkins for her Malta photos, and to Sue for her line drawings and photos.

Table of Contents

A Death Proves to Be Only the Beginning

1 'Get Over Here!'

The call from my farmer-in-law was not only rarer than hen's teeth. It was also exquisitely badly timed.

I have a confession to get out of the way. I am world champion at prevaricating. There is no urgent job, no pile of marking, no lesson preparation, no set of reports to concoct, check or summarise, no assembly to write that cannot be left until the last minute, or rather later. Lo and behold, half term was looming, and a few more hours of vacillation, pen sorting, desk paper shuffling and all the other well-oiled diversionary distractions and I could postpone the pile for another week and sit awkwardly on the guilt.

The Memsahib's fearsome father was a man of few spare words, even by farmers' standards. I instantly offered to get the boss, his favourite daughter, (she has two younger brothers) but the shock intensified.

"No, it's you I want to talk to. Can you get over here now? I can't cope." I needed a seat. I get on well enough with Jim Chalybeate, but he is never normally tongue tied when pointing out my lack of farm skills or practical knowledge, or any other shortcomings. The brain froze. If he wants my help, it certainly can't be anything agricultural.

"Where are you?" I played for time.

"Back at the flat, otherwise I couldn't be phoning you, fool. I have just come from the hospital. It is awful. Can you and Rosy come out tomorrow?" Ah. Do I listen to the in-laws' family updates carefully? Of course not.

Rack brain. Jim's parents retired to Malta. His mum passed away some while ago. Granddad Chalybeate and sons, Jim and Ed, never got on with their dad. Mr C senior had been poorly for a while.

"Yes, fine. I'll get on to a travel agent. See you in Malta tomorrow, with a bit of luck, with Rosy and little Anne, who will be six months next week. I'll pass you on to Rosy."

When she put the phone down, Rosy was half tearful, half furious.

"Dad's in a mess. Not because of Granddad's dying, but because of his Will.

"I'll start packing. Can't we go today?"

2 Not a Fun Journey

Travelling in haste with a six-month-old daughter is a bit fraught. I like understatement. Changing planes in Rome was the first shock. Air Malta had a relaxed approach to seating reservations, and a gloriously simple smoking policy: seats on the left could not, those on the right seemed required to. Naturally, the smoke declined to cross the narrow aisle. Great with a babe in arms. By Easter, the Med is already a lot warmer than northern Europe. Once landed, the race to get out was a free for all, with no quarter given or asked. When we eventually reached the door and turned left, the blast furnace heat and new smells hit the face, as the trousers stuck to the legs, and Anne started screaming. Acclimatisation consisted of standing in the sun on the apron for twenty minutes while our folding pushchair was found.

Jim met us, and all five piled into Granddad's immaculate, well preserved anyway, two-tone Wolseley 16/60, complete with Burgundy red leather seats. Think Austin Cambridge, plus a posh grille with a lit up logo in it. Class! Also, car sickness from the slow soft springs battling the hard fast rutted roads, and my father-in-law smoking to ease his blood pressure in the island's manic traffic. It is not anarchic, merely that our genes can't decode the rules. Same highway code, but treated as desiderata, not obligation, same side of the road, but only by narrow fluctuating majority.

(1) Timeless, endless traffic

Not a man for superfluous small talk, some light chat was needed, in between motoring expletives, as we headed for the hospital. But we soon hit the only issue.

13

"I'm glad you've got here. I don't think he'll last today or tomorrow at the longest. He may recognise you, but I doubt it. He was about lucid when I arrived last week, but not for the couple of days that could have saved this ungodly mess."

Jim wasn't wrong. We reached a frail and barely conscious old man, whose life was ebbing away. He didn't see Rosy but perked up a bit when he heard her voice and seemed to smile when Anne cried the once. Jim remained stony faced.

However, much one was needed, and apposite, there were no death bed confessions, more's the pity.

3 A Disaster in Prospect

We didn't stay long, and braved the coast road back to the flat, on Bugibba's cliff edge, overlooking St Paul's Bay.

Once in and with a large Scotch in hand, Jim started talking, and shaking, and crying.

"The miserable old…" he couldn't articulate the words, but what he meant was clear enough. "Instead of leaving his and Grandma's flat and whatever to your uncle Ed and me, he's left it all to some Gold Digger bleach blond barmaid from Bradford!"

I poured myself a large Scotch too, and even Rosy broke her nursing embargo with a glass of wine. She regretted it quickly, not because of Anne, but because Malta's legendary plonk, 'Lachryma Vitis' does indeed bring tears to the eyes.

4 One Passing, Much Starting

Early next morning, the hospital phoned, to say Granddad had, as expected, not lasted the night. Jim managed to, shall we say, keep his grief well under control. It made for a busy day, and longer in the Wolseley than anyone would have liked. First to the hospital, 'The Mater Dei' (Mother of God), close enough to Valetta to be clagged with traffic, to sort the essential forms, all foolscap brown paper, clumsily printed pro formas with wobbly black lines, and over wordy Maltese and English (in Italics) Times Roman. Most empires have invaded Malta down the centuries. The British were last to go and left behind 1950s' vintage sepia tinted bureaucracy.

Then back inland to Mosta, away from any sort of qualified modernity, and into glorious timelessness. The car had to be left on the edge of the old town, and we made our way through the tight, camel coloured, dull and dusty little lanes, framed by tall dusty raw limestone or plastered walls. We reached a dull, old, nearly decrepit gate, about three metres tall, and Jim pulled the stiff wrought iron bell handle. I was confused. Why were we in this tatty run-down part of town, when visiting a top lawyer? My mind set's settings were awry.

(2) Dr Grech's doorway (SAH)

The great gate creaked open, to reveal a dry, dusty old lawyer, or so it seemed. When he saw Jim, his face opened up to a charming smile and a courteous greeting. His courtyard was in total contrast to outside. A full oasis of shady glades, hanging grapes and kiwis (the fruit), ripe lemons, exotic potted flowers and aromatic herbs. An assortment of fountains twinkled and splashed leisurely. Watching over them were a series of statues, in classical poses and dress, all looking as if they could be blessed back into life with a deft touch.

"Lesley Grech. Delighted to meet you, Rosy and husband Iain, I take it, and this must by your new addition... Anne, is it?"

He bent to shake hands, with his right, while a pair of gardening clippers rested in his left.

"I was hoping to get a spot of pruning done before you arrived," he said as he ushered us in, and gently swung the hefty gate back shut. "Come on in. I should have realised. Right on time. Here in Malta, we have two systems: British time and Maltese time. The former is what you expect – punctuality and precision, expectation, hurry and stress. The latter is more Mediterranean. We know things will happen, but God or the fates often conspire to cause delays. We borrow 'Insha'Allah', if God wills it, from the Arabs, and 'Mañana', tomorrow, meaning in reality 'not today' from the Spanish. We get there in the end. You decide which works best. In your own time, of course!"

5 Maltese Law, in Person

How to describe, nay, encapsulate the character, ambience…ah, aura, that's the word. Suffice it to say, if the estimable John Mortimer had been looking for a role model for his most famous creation, he could have written every word of Rumpole in Villa Grech-Mifsud. Perhaps he did.

Dr Grech's office is taller than wide and stacked to the ceiling with dusty legal books. His desk is in there, somewhere, under mountains of scrolled and escaping papers. It is gloriously timeless. Most of the world's legal history is catalogued therein, somewhere. Maybe not the latest trendy stuff, but certainly most of the Henrys' divorce papers, co-respondents Caesar J v Anthony M v Patra C, The Solicitors' Guide to Domestic Pharmacology from the Borgias to

Crippen, and many other sedimentarily enveloped once-bestselling tomes. One volume did catch my eye, being freshly thumbed and devoid of dust, 'The Maltese Law of Usufruct', of which more anon.

"Do sit down, do sit down, all of you," beamed the good Doctor (LLB), before realising this wasn't practicable, and leaping up with surprising agility rehoused three tottering piles of briefs (legal) on to fresh albeit stale multi-storey abodes, temporarily, maybe.

We sat, with confidence; the chairs were dust free, and would have considered our weight trivial after the weighty tomes now evicted. Rosy was fully occupied with Anne, who wanted to explore, but could not be allowed much freedom of movement, as the evidence suggested that Malta was not then up to speed on EU health and safety norms.

"First, my sympathies for your loss, Jim, and family." His tone was suitably serious, but there was no mistaking the light twinkle in his eye, giving us—if spotted—the first inkling that not everything in ink was inviolate. "You'll be here about the...ahem... 'Last Will and Testament' of your late Father, Richard, known to most as Dickie, for one reason or another." Jim's blood pressure was peaking.

"It's a bloody disgrace!"

"Mr Chalybeate, I do understand you're upset. But bear with me. The picture is possibly a little more complex, and a lot less alarming than it might appear. There is much to discuss. Am I right in thinking that you are enlisting the help of Iain, your son in law, in going through the legal maze?" He gave a kindly and knowing nod in my direction.

"Aye, that's about it. He'll have to do, if there's no one better available." It was a well-rehearsed line, insult once, cliché later, family in-joke before now.

"But what do you mean? That b**** gets the 'misuse as fact' or whatever you called it of all my money for as long as she lives, damn her. And the bloody lot if I tell her to go and stuff the Will. What's the point of doing anything?"
Jim was not best pleased.

"Mr Chalybeate, hear me out, in good time. As I will explain, there is hope yet. All is not necessarily as it seems. My advice is that you do indeed challenge and reject your father's Will!" Now, there was a puckish glint in Dr Grech's voice, as well as eye.

"But we will have to resume tomorrow. You all need to get to the cemetery.

"You British have taught us many things, but, sadly, I fear we are ahead of you in matters of sclerotic traffic. Again, my sympathies and consolations. I hope the interment is peaceful."

6 Burial Without Closure

We were up early again next morning, and back across the island once more in the trusty Wolseley. Given Malta's heat, all burials must be within the day following death. We got to the cemetery, Santa Maria Addolorata, meaning dedicated to Holy Mary of the Sorrows. Did I mention that Malta is deeply and visibly Catholic, through and through? That guides their customs and behaviour, and of course inspires the architecture.

Don't think of a British lawn lined with trees, and calm refreshing green. Malta is not the place to go for immaculate grass – too hot, too dry. Also, space is tight and the hill side is packed solid with graves, memorials, crypts and vaults, all in hot, reflective stone, engraved and usually with artificial flowers, themselves wilting in the heat.

(3a) Santa Maria Addolorata Graveyard, Valetta

Despite being tightly packed, they are still running out of room, and are 're-dedicating' the older spots.

The ceremony was brief to the point of being perfunctory. Jim's father was laid to rest with his late wife, Agnes, who had preceded him by a short decade. The priest and attendant gravedigger were thanked, in hand. We left in silence, bar the tune of a few flies, who themselves only seemed to be going through the motions of expected duty.

(3b) The Cemetery Entrance (SAH)

We all had an overwhelming sense of inadequacy, of being diddled, by each in turn of the lack of mourning time, the Spartan ceremony, and by the impending and expanding problems relating to the Will.

Death is not the end – in this case, only the beginning. I am sure I have read those words before. Any help? Leaving earthly cares is only a release for one.

Simply pain without rest for the rest.

We need to go back in time for a while to see how we got to be by that dry and deathly space. If you think time should only go in one direction, or even at a vaguely predictable speed, you have not been to Malta.

2 The Founding of the Chalybeate Dynasty: Yorkshire and Lancashire in Union

We must leave the Chalybeates marooned between cemetery, the late Granddad's flat and Dr Grech's legal nest, and tease out the threads of how the family got there. Given Malta's traffic, which appears to be more still life than poetry in motion, that seems an appropriate place to leave them, in suspended animation, not to mention suspense of how the deepening crisis will evolve. Also frozen in time*, again, as parts of Malta often appear to be. *Maybe sun-dried in time is closer than frozen, by more than a few degrees.

1 Bradford Antebellum

Not for the last time, we have to leave the warmth of the Mediterranean's sunshine and go back in time to rather less sunny Bradford, as it is in several senses the literal Garden of…no, I can't finish that… Garden of Origin, maybe? Of this evolving narrative.

The industrial West Riding of Yorkshire sits on top of immense coal reserves and under fewer clouds than Lancashire, on the drier leeward side of the Pennines. As a result, the light has its own quality (restored now the coal mining and coal burning industries have all but ceased) sharp, clear and with a bright, hard edge. You might relate this to key attributes of the local character: hard work and willingness to get the hands dirty below; sharp bright and unyielding above. True Yorkshiremen certainly do, with little hesitation or invitation, but with plenty of repetition and critical comparison.

They do not suffer fools gladly, if at all, and will tell you such.

The good folk of Bradford may have to follow in step to more prosperous and upmarket Leeds, but they will play second fiddle to precious few others. All are fiercely independent and have a clear sense of what's right and what's wrong. They are right, and you can suit yourself.

I mention this not because of my interest in all things geographical, but because there is little doubt that the formative years' environment—social and climatic—has an effect on character development. No less so with Mr Chalybeate, senior and junior(s).

Policing this sturdy race is not for the faint hearted. It is a happy valley, in its own fashioning of the phrase. If charged with looking after and keeping order among hard, unyielding and self-determining people, the officer in uniform needs to be, to coin a phrase, cut from similarly sturdy and resilient cloth.

2 Formative Years

Granddad, then just young Richard Chalybeate, began on the beat in Bradford, and nearby Baildon. Too facile to say the Police force made him the man he was; more likely he and the uniform were made for each other.

Like much in life, chance and happenstance played some key cards. Richard Chalybeate was born in Bradford in late 1903. He turned 14 at the end of 1917, when victory on the Western Front was by no means assured, and was made sharply less so by the sudden Russian collapse in the East. The Army recruiting team took an interest, and he was soon in cadet uniform, undergoing very basic training.

But by the time he and his peers were pronounced ready for 'Dulce et Decorum Est', the tide finally turned, and they were never sent to France, and were demobbed even before The Armistice. But the cumulative wastage of working men's manpower bade ill for rebuilding the economy. The police were as short staffed as anyone and encouraging young men to swap khaki for midnight blue was an obvious part solution. Richard jumped at the chance.

The uniform conferred status and financial stability, a step up to be put to good use. He was still in his teens when he started 'walking out' with and then courting a Miss Agnes Thwaite, and they wed with the family's blessing.

(4) Relatives in uniform, c.1918

The Thwaites were a class or two clear of the Chalybeates then, but the uniform and 'prospects' bridged the gap. They were from around what later became known as The Golden Triangle, and dabbled in a number of areas, including housing for rent and shopkeeping. Both would turn out to come in handy decades later on.

PC Chalybeate R made the grade on foot patrol, and was promoted to the mounted squad. He was a good horseman and treated his steeds with a kindness and care he didn't always lavish on his family. But all good things must come to an end. When Jim and later Ed(ward) came along, and a pensionable early exit door opened, they were through it at P38 Lightning speed. (Relax! It's an aviation joke). Where else to go but Bradford-on-Sea, also known as Morecambe.

3 From Yorkshire to Lancashire

Like many seaside resorts, Morecambe was the creation of the railway, the revolution that allowed the slaves of the Great Wen industrial towns to give the lungs a week or two's breather, each annual summer Wakes Week. Leeds' Tykes to Bridlington and Scarborough, Brummies to Weston Super Mare, Scousers to Rhyl and Llandudno, Manks to Blackpool, Cockneys to Margate…and much of Bradford to Morecambe.

(5) Morecambe front & beach. Tide in = rare photo

Know the old railway map, and you know the lines of escape. As the railways gave, so the charter flights and budget airlines took away: with reliable sunshine the Mediterranean coast ripped the heart out of both holiday and retirement residences along the British littoral. This exodus was eventually to include the by then retired senior Chalybeates, and their life savings. When a riding accident, while in uniform, offered Sgt Chalybeate an early pension,

Morecambe was the obvious destination. Dickie's lump sum supplied the capital to buy 'The Harbour Guest House', on the front, in Morecambe's West End, and Agnes took the greater share of the hotelling duties, at least during her husband's convalescence. The fresh air was a blessing. Not that parents or boys will have noticed all that much – all four were heavy smokers all their lives, except Dickie, who managed to kick the addiction in his rejuvenated Maltese days.

4 Farming Is Better than School

Young Jim did well enough in the classroom but tended to learn largely what might come in handy as soon as he could be out of the school gate and in through a field gate. Ed was the same, but usually got an advantage over his big brother by skipping the wasted school part of the day completely. Both boys loved the coast, the sand, the rock pools, fishing, collecting eggs (it was not frowned upon in those days). The Constabulary Cavalry gene passed from father to sons. Both got weekend jobs mucking out stables, and Jim was quickly promoted to stable lad, and earned tidy pocket money exercising racehorses across the endless flat sands. Endless at low tide, that is – nothing at all at high tide, and great skill and local knowledge were always needed to keep clear of the inrushing tide.

Younger Ed made do with odd jobs and stable cleaning, less well paid, but a better earner as he was often scraping—literally—his pocket money (fag cash) while Jim was in class.

Both boys left school at 14, and it was soon time for Dickie and Agnes to start again. Jim left school with a good certificate at the then normal leaving age; Ed parted company with formal education in an appropriately casual and intermittent manner, at an unrecorded age. Both boys had not the slightest interest in urban or indoor careers, so Dickie again cashed up, and took a huge risk by ploughing it all into a farm, an activity he had not the slightest training for, bar his horse experience.

(6) Jim Chalybeate in his early days farming in the Lune Valley

This was, however, key. Pre-WW2 farms were almost entirely horse-powered, certainly on England's pastoral west side. Indeed, the number of tractors did not overtake that of horses until years after that war, no doubt accelerated both by wartime losses of horses and tank factories being able to convert to tractor production.

The Chalybeates' new dairy and sheep farm was in the lush Lune Valley – drought not being a common problem, the grass is verdant, when not sodden. It is still there, greatly enlarged, horseless, and with more tractors than they started with cows. Jim and Edward both married local girls, with farm experience. In due course, Jim took over at home, and Edward settled round the corner. In a curious circling of coincidence, one field was later sold off to the leisure horseyculture riding sector, so there are again nags on the lane.

(7) The Original Grey Ferguson (Later MF 35),
still working today

As the farms established themselves – 'prospered' is a dangerous word and could only really claim to have been (well) earned after decades of toil – and Dickie and Agnes aged, one more career beckoned, as did their native Yorkshire.

They bought a traditional and well reputed sweet shop in Knaresborough, and Agnes rediscovered her family talent for property, and an assortment of bargain terraces swelled their portfolio. Need you ask: yes, of course these have bit parts to play in our story, when it returns to relatively recent days, and relative squabbles.

The sweetshop thrived, in the days when Knaresborough enjoyed an upmarket cachet, and before supermarkets swamped, nay drowned, the craft shop on the high street.

Their collection of houses produced some sort of income and offered the promise of capital security.

(8) Knaresborough in its heyday

But the retail business was starting to slow down, and bespoke sweet making clearly losing out to the mass marketed brands, when Dickie and Agnes hit retirement age, and they sold up for the last time, left their sons and families to it and headed for the sun.

Time to Invade Malta

1 Looking for Warmth

Where best? In the late 1960s, the options were opening up, but not that much. Needing an English speaking and sympathetic environment, an affordable and short flight, with a cheap cost of living narrowed the odds, for the Chalybeates and many other retirees, to Gibraltar, Malta and Cyprus.

At least in part because of the shop, Agnes and Dickie had for a few years taken staggered holidays. Agnes had proved surprisingly adventurous and headed off on 'banana boat' cheap cruises, on freight boats that had a few spare cabins for intrepid explorers. She was not put off by a few surprises in diet, customs or local mores. Dickie and mates had sampled the delights of Malta a few times. The family's collective oral archive and memories recall very little of his adventures, which is maybe for the better.

Off they went, as well prepared as most of the sun-seeking silver-haired diaspora. How many Brits have hatched plans to swap our well-soaked island for a sun-soaked paradise? You have, we have (and have). But if that starter answer is unquantifiable, so must the follow up be: seventh heaven or seventh circle of hell on earth?

Our dreams are in sun warmed stones, shaded balconies with azure seas seen through ice-rich cocktail prisms, elegantly perspiring by the pool side; but our wakings are anxious sweaty exchange rate checkings, and waiting for cheque-ins, opaque and always draining local bills, framed in impenetrable local legalese, exquisitely crafted and grafted specifically to promote paranoia in the sunset era expat.

Malta, showing key locations in the story

2 Why Malta?

Post-colonial British retirees seeking sunshine in their sunset years are hardly the first army to try their luck on Maltese shores. Most invaders brought, and left with, mixed blessings.

You, being a keen student of Mediterranean ancient history, archaeology, ethnography, linguistic and cultural conflict and assimilation, C20th nationalism and geopolitics; with side dishes in the empirics of Empirical expansion and decline…can skip a few pages. Our heroes, or at least the Saga sagas of the Chalybeate dynasty, are taking a break, as they don't get much mention in Malta's first few thousand years of pre and printed history. But we have sneaked in a few maps and sketches to tickle the interest. Come and enjoy a tardy, but Tardis-free, free potted picture of Malta though all its ages…before the Great Chalybeate arrival.

3 Malta: CV

All but the irredeemably incarterate will instantly spot the obvious key geographical significance of the Maltese archipelago, with Gozo and Comino, little sisters next door: North-South right between North African/Maghreb and European/Italian peoples and cultures; East-West half way along the Med, between the Atlantic at Gibraltar and the Red Sea at Suez. Strategically vital, since boats and even aircraft were invented.

You, aspirant Imperial Emperor of the Greater Med, you have very little chance of getting the job done without controlling Gib, Malta, Alex, and Cyprus. 'Good Luck', say those lesser generals, Hannibal, Marc Anthony, Napoleon, Musso and Rommel, inter alia (or is that inter-Axis?), all of whom have tried and failed.

Culturally, you cannot beat the melting pot. The Maltese language is of Arabic origin, written in our (Roman) script, though with rather more QQs and XXs than we are used to. Half the words come from Italian, and the rest from Arabic, English and French. Confused? You should be, and I am only warming up.

The three islands have a combined area of only just over 300 km^2, which is under half that of Singapore, and you could fit them into London four times, and still have room for a garden or two. As for people, that gets more interesting. Half a million live there, so a mere twentieth of London. But there are more Maltese in Melbourne, Australia, than on the island, and plenty more still in the world's other great cities. The Maltese originated as sailors, and the wanderlust has never left them. I think you are safe to say that globally, the Maltese have made more of an impact than their numbers suggest.

4 A Long and Proud Past

How much Maltese archaeology, history and culture do you need? None, if all you are doing is having a fortnight of sun, sea, sand and so on, with each day's memories glugged away with milk of amnesia. But rather more is essential in order to live and soak up the ambiance. The Maltese will expect and appreciate your sense of empathy and getting yourself into the right mind set and knowing the background context. They are very proud of their history.

Malta is a flat limestone plateau, with a strong sun and weak rain. There are no permanent rivers, and water is always scarce. The soils are thin, and farming is tough. But the waters teem with fish and offer trade to everywhere of everything. So, sailing and trading are in the blood.

Sicily is only 90 km away, and the first settlers came from there, some 6000 years ago. They brought pottery, seeds and flint tools. They had a good run of 2000 years and built simple rock temples. But even before Jesus was born, there were four more invasions—from bronze and then iron using peoples. Then the Phoenicians sailed in, still only 800BC, coming in their sleek trading boats from their Holy Land or via their outpost at Carthage on the now Tunisian coast. Next along, the Romans. Malta prospered, thanks to new technologies, such as good pottery and weaving, and trade through the great natural harbours.

St Paul was shipwrecked, probably in 'St Paul's Bay', of which the Chalybeate's flat in Bugibba is a part, west of Valetta, in 60AD. This is mentioned in the Bible, 'Acts of the Apostles' and backed up by archaeological digging. In the 9th Century, the Arabs invaded, and established their capital at the hilltop Mdina. They brought Islam and the water wheel, great for irrigated farming. Yet more invasions, by Normans and others led eventually to the Knights of St John moving home to Malta, after the Crusades, and via Cyprus and Rhodes.

Most Maltese have been staunch Catholics ever since.

(9) The Great Siege of 1565 – the definitive history

One of Malta's two great siege battles took up most of 1565, when the Ottoman Turks were expanding, and saw Malta as the prefect staging post for conquering the western Mediterranean. 48,000 well-armed troops, with excellent artillery, overran most of the island, and besieged Valetta and Mdina, with only 8000 defenders. They held out for a full month, in the blasting heat, with endless dust from the bombardment, and the Knights wearing their own weight in steel armour. The Ottoman victory was short lived, only until reinforcements arrived from Sicily, and history did not need to be re-written.

The Knights lasted until when they were running out of energy and money, the French invaded in 1798. Napoleon's army's arrival of course attracted the British who evicted their then enemy almost immediately and stayed until full independence in the 1970s.

But having a base in Malta proved absolutely vital again during the Second World War, 1939–45.

(10) Gloster Gladiator. Photo by Bae

Malta was a vital refuelling stop for British RAF planes getting to the front in Egypt. The Axis powers lacked food and especially oil. They needed to get to Middle East oil. Malta was attacked continuously, from June 1940 to the end of 1942. Losses were terrible, on both sides, land, sea and air. Valletta was evacuated under the bombing. At one point, the defensive air force was reduced to three pre-war Gladiator bi-planes, nicknamed 'Faith', 'Hope' and 'Charity', the first of which, and only survivor, is on display in the national museum. In April 1942, King George VI awarded The George Cross Medal to the whole island, and it remains on the national flag today.

(11) RAF Beaufighter at Ta'Qali, 27 June 1943, 272 Sqdn Note Mdina behind.

After the war, the British naval base was one of the main sources of employment, but a shrinking UK presence and independence meant Malta had to look for other ways to make a living. This has been successful.

Manufacturing, especially textiles and electronics, is surprisingly important for a small island with no energy supplies or resources, as is trade and shipping.

Tourism leads the way, thanks to a great location, English being spoken by almost everyone, guaranteed sunshine and clear blue warm seas.

For the same reasons, film making is popular, and the set of 'Popeye' has been kept as an attraction. Most tourists enjoy the quick package tours and flights, the ones that killed Morecambe and Skegness. Some, like our Dickie and Agnes, stay, put down roots, and as the quick become the dead, will be part of Maltese soil for eternity.

5 Dreams Meet Realities

Idyllic is the dream. The reality is seldom so simple. The Chalybeates (generation upon generation) are excellent budget managers and take care to be 19s6d creditors rather than 20s6d debtors. But even the best calculations are only estimates, and Macmillanesque 'events' conspire, as Wodehouse put it, to be hiding round the corner, filling a swinging sock with lead. Then as now, the British Government's habit of selling off capital assets to make current budgets meet fails to create the genuine wealth (for the proles) that finances pensions...or supports the Pound.

When Dickie and Agnes took their pensions (and their Bradford and Baildon terraced house rental trickles) to Malta, one imperial Pound Sterling was worth roughly one Maltese Lira. By the late 1970s, it took over £1.60 to get a Lira: pensions down by a third. With no oil, and most food imported, Maltese prices were not immune to inflation. Fixed income retired Expats felt the pinch. Family visiting trips back to Blighty dropped rapidly in frequency, although if you caught Dickie, Jim or Ed in mid refill and without an eary wall, each might not have lamented this lengthening wavelength. On the farm, Jim's boys were growing into the job, and didn't always value technical advice from a freshly minted 1950s mindset. Agnes had her own solution, and took to her wheelchair, with blanket, on arrival in Manchester; only later to reveal the gallon bottle of Bell's between her knees, the benefits of which passed No.11 Downing Street's greedy eagle eyes by.

Equally entrepreneurial Dickie rarely lacked an eye for any chance, economic, social or amorous. He took risks of all sorts, including explosive, by finding ways to circumvent his reverent Catholic hosts' strict Sunday observance laws. Retiring in the sunshine became increasingly relative, not absolute.

6 Not a Bad Sunset

For all that, Agnes and Dickie made a decent life in Bugibba. Without, we think, ever getting any more of the local lingo than the imported 'Insha'Allah', used by Dickie well past the point of irritation, they made friends, good and definitely ungood, and mixed into parts of local life.

(12) The Swordfish Restaurant and Bar, St Paul's Bay (SAH)

Several evenings a week saw both at 'The Swordfish' bar restaurant grill and disco, above the quay, and only a ten-minute stroll from the flat. Agnes could enjoy a social smoke, a small glass of weak beer and a large glass of Scotch, while Dickie acted in a combined role of opportunist, fixer and middleman. In truth, he was more Elderly Dell Boy than thrusting local Alan Sugar (or is that Alan 'Zokkor'?) but it amused him and his 'business associates', as they watered down their profits by the bar (and feasted their watering eyes on the younger disco aficionados' perambulations).

Agnes' health stabilised in the warm air, but no more. She was not too mobile and did not drive. When the weather was not too torrid, Dickie and Agnes did their fair share of exploring the island in the trusty Wolseley, and even got across to Gozo on occasion. At home, she looked after the flat, and pottered down to the quay. Armed with a motorised wheelchair, she could explore bits of Bugibba and St Paul's Bay and get herself up the hill to the Doctor's surgery, which was in his spacious and elegant villa, overlooking the bay. This latter became more frequent both as she aged, and as he became her principal source of advice, support and encouragement.

The old domed church next door but one was also a destination in itself – cool, beautiful, restful, timeless. She visited both, up to within a few weeks of her last trip to hospital in May 1980.

Meanwhile, Dickie's misadventures expanded, and supplied him with questionable extra cash, thrills and the illusion of importance in the community. Although the net financial benefit of all his wheeling and dealing was invariably negative, it seemed not to exercise the Excise or the Uniformed Branches of local law.

We lack any material evidence, or witness statements, but it is plausible to infer that Dickie would have been busy ingratiating himself with his former profession; that they found this amusing, and trivial; and in all probability that they themselves may have benefited (hardly 'profited') from his shady if not really dark activities.

Dickie's impromptu quay-level garage market, barter and gossip node would also have been a handy hangout for an alert policeman's ear, in mufti, of course.

7 Flat Facts and Garage Capitalism

Ah. An embarrassing lacuna. All this time, you have been thinking that all the Malta Chalybeates have been homeless or at best merely existing when not out and about. Far from it. Dickie and Agnes bought 'Sorrento', Flat no.4, 2nd Floor, Harbour Road, Bugibba as soon as they had got organised in Malta. Being on the fairly steep incline between corniche and quay helped the builders. The main entrance was on the ridge roadside, and only a storey and a half of stairs to the second floor. But by descending to the end and turning back, the garage, subterranean from the front, opened onto shore level.

Like many 1950s blocks of flats, the architecture was nothing special to look at. Inside, tiles and clean walls were more than adequate. The structure was solid, the fittings tolerable if clearly dated by the time we saw it. Decorations were on the sparse side, partly hand-me-downs and souvenirs from Bradford and Morecambe, and partly seaside tat. Books gathered little dust, there being very few about.

The great storyteller Anton Chekov—who am I to question his diktat—insists that the pistol on the wall must not be mentioned, unless it is fired as part of the plot. So, I am constrained not to embellish the story, or the walls, with any bourgeois décor details, until they become necessary. Sorry about that.

Immediately, therefore, the balcony hoves into the mind's eye. No great elegance graced it, but no matter. The tiled floor seemed steady enough, although sand, cigarette butts and small, loose, curly edged carpet scraps always invited a trip, a balcony somersault and a premature end, on the garage's apron far enough below. The open terrace was boxed in with glazed panels, some fixed, some sliding, some fixed but designed to slide. Aluminium cannot rust, but these managed the idea. Even closed, the balcony could be chill on an out of season night; even open it could be very sweaty when the summer sun came visiting.

Think me not churlish, all can be forgiven for the view. Vertically below, Dickie's hive of activity; beyond that, a crazy pavement of waterfront commerce and leisure—boats on and off trailers, water skis and flippers akimbo, pier- and boat-based fishermen and all their tackle; small commercial fishing boats, with slimy, drying, holed, mending, float and weight adorned edges; speedboats with engines itching for the off, static boats with engines ashore; spectators, helpers, tourists, couples making out, small boys making mayhem, and lots of flotsam that was now jetsam, animal, vegetable and mineral. It is better than it reads, but Steinbeck I ain't.

Beyond all that, the blue, blue water, speckled with boats, skiers, sailors, all framed by headlands and horizons. At night, the same in cobalt, framed by thin random selections of speckly street lamps around the shores and ever denser patterns of stars above.

An endless kaleidoscopic light show and Lowryesque moving pattern, by day or night; all to be enjoyed from the seeming serenity of the second (or is it fourth) storey above the garage petrol bomb.

Being a devout country, there is no trading on the Sabbath. Hedonistic tourists want their Funday. Fishermen don't believe the fish deserve a break, even after Friday. Smugglers hope the Police are at church. All need petrol, spare parts, odd bits of kit. Dickie's basement garage has never welcomed a car or boat, not a full one, but it was home to any number of bits of many, not to mention tackle, ropes, buoys, rods, poles and perches. Mostly, though, it had lots of jerry cans of petrol.

A hot climate, careless users in a hurry, mostly smokers, underneath a block of flats. What could possibly go wrong? The flats are still there. What did go wrong was Dickie's pricing policy. Instead of holy day usury, he let himself get conned at 'mates' rates' prices: he was ripped off, when the juice was not actually being stolen. Life and soul of the quayside, that Dickie, and cheaper than retail. Being a pal, at a price.

Being a monopoly supplier of bargain basement priced petrol made Sundays a social time underneath Sorrento. Time is of the essence, as the French say.

8 Dickie's Chicks and Self-Harming Bodyguards

I have struggled to uncover objective confirmation of this cameo tale. Neither have I reason to declare it untrue. Judge for yourself. This is how it has been related to me, with some consistency.

Most of the Chalybeate clan visited Sorrento at some point or other. Few went a second time. Rose was the exception. She was, and is, a slave to duty. But she also wanted to keep in touch with her Nana, especially in the latter's declining years. Being a student and then a PE teacher of limited means also meant that a spot of summer beach time in the summer holidays had its attractions. The flight was gladly sponsored by Jim and Mum, as it bailed them out of any lingering responsibility for leaving the farm in hay time and ticked the family visit box.

One fine July, Rose took two of her best friends, Joy and Gail, from PE College days with her. Mostly, they had a good week. They could borrow the Wolseley for a few mornings and dutifully see the guidebook essentials. The same again for the odd evening's expedition to Bugibba's discos, away from The Swordfish, where the ancients' presence cloistered any possible hedonism. It was worth the breakfast interrogation as to where they had been, Dickie having assiduously checked the milometer readings.

But of course, afternoons in the saltwater pool or on the beach were the main attraction, along with flippers, snorkels and all the other littoral clutter. Being PE specialists, all were of course naturals on water skis. Finding a willing speedboat, or to be exact, a willing speedboat driver, with boat, was Dickie's self-appointed mission, and he loved it.

The girls came to be known as 'Dickie's Chicks', out of their earshot, of course. PE athletes, Joy among them, tend to have an educated left foot, and Gail had a polished and practised right hook, though in fairness, that caused mere contusions compared to her whiplash tongue, when needed. Aerosol Mace is only for wimps. Dickie basked in the adulation, wholly missing the withering sarcasm in the appellation.

He bumped into the right pair, or more accurately, a right pair, Messrs. Yusef and Iskander, who were loitering around the flashier end of the port. A couple of Libyans there is no big deal. It is not much further south to the Maghreb coast of Africa than it is north to Italy. He didn't presume to ask why one of them, Iskander, I am told, had his arm in plaster.

"Hello boys! Salaam whatsit." Dickie gave them his broadest smile. "Here for a bit of power boating and water skiing?"

The reply was distinctly cautious. Upfront straight to the point interrogation is normal practice in Yorkshire; highly suspicious in the lesser, larger, rest of the world. "Err… Yes, thanking you. We are making holiday in your nice Malta. This our boat, but petrol short. This Jo, I Alex – we friends already, so be pleased to use short form of classical names, yes?"

Even better, thought Dickie. "Boys, we can kill two birds with one stone here!"

Both Libyans flinched at the word 'kill', before failing to get to grips with the peculiar English idiom.

"If I sell you some petrol, half price, would you take these three lovely ladies water skiing?"

Both men looked at each other. What kind of a trick is this? Where's the catch? Can this man be such a complete idiot? They shrugged and decided he could be. This was a nice risk compared to the usual. The Eid was last week, but today was clearly Christmas.

(13) Rosy water-skiing in St Paul's Bay. Note the Malta flag.

'Dickie's Chicks' were considerably less enamoured of the scheme, the boat, the story and the consequences. But they felt cornered by their host's hospitality. With some reluctance, and measuring the odds of three against one and a half, given the inactive right arm, and being very keen on the skiing, they climbed in.

An hour or so later, the three sports ladies had had a decent crack each; and the two men had enjoyed their status. Way out in the bay, the kit was reeled in, and the boat headed back, as slowly as Yusef could make it. If you believe their chat up line, the men were bodyguards for the then and well-known Libyan Leader. They were on leave, while Isk… 'Call me Alex, we now friends' was recuperating, after being shot. So, he said. A flesh wound was unwrapped as trophy exhibit. Whether he had taken one for his leader, in the line of fire on duty, or during an off-duty domestic was not explained.

The girls voted 3-0 for the latter.

They did search 'The Times of Malta' and last week's London Sunday papers when back in Bugibba, but assassination attempts were conspicuous by their absence in the columns.

"We meet again, this evening, maybe, yes?" enquired Jo, pushing his luck.

"Which is best bar in area?"

"The Swordfish, look, you can see it now," replied Joy, while Gail pointed emphatically at the building, with its blue neon, vaguely fishy illumination, while smiling with equally temporary simulated enthusiasm.

No need to discuss or articulate the obvious plan. This was easier than seeing off aspiringly amorous trainee teachers. Being courted by bodyguards doesn't make for lasting relationships, especially as our Yusuf and Iskander were evidently not very good at their vocations.

At sunset, at the hour agreed, the Wolseley headed briskly… East, for a peaceful drink in suddenly safe seeming Sliema, half way to Valletta.

9 New Life as a Widower

Enough cameos of senior citizen life in exile. Time ticked along, and Agnes' health declined. She died not so long after Rosy's last visit. With her passing, the flow of news from Bugibba dried up too. The detective work starts. More will emerge later, but in outline, it would seem that Dickie's mourning period was at the shorter end of respectable.

He adapted to second bachelorhood with little remorse, and seems to have extended his social circle, in The

Swordfish, around the garage and among both the transient and rooted expat communities along the north coast. He might have had more liaisons, but it is clear that one particular friendship tickled his fancy.

We will meet Ms Marigold again later. She hailed from Bradford, too. Whether their coming together was complete coincidence, or whether their mutually acceptable accents made them a natural pairing is not now checkable. What does seem certain is that they became at least a part time 'item', and her visits happened more often, and without the need for inclusive packages.

At any rate, not long before Rosy re-entered the story, and I made my first unwitting ('witless, more like' I can hear Jim chipping in) entrance, Dickie went to see Dr Grech, and 'update' his will.

Secrets of the Maltese Legal Eagle's Nest

This takes us back to Mosta, and forward to the then present day in time. We had left Jim, Rosy, Anne and me in the Wolseley heading back to Bugibba and the flat. Rosy made a brew and sorted Anne's tea out, while Jim had a smoke on the balcony, and stared out across port and bay. I offered him a snifter, it being a more or less respectable time, but to my surprise he said he wanted out of the flat.

We walked down to The Swordfish and dined there. I had just that, Jim ate a shark, and Rosy went for a safe white fish. None of us could remember what any of it tasted like. Being midweek, and pre-season, the disco wasn't working, and only the very regulars were in, mostly at the bar. Jim refilled his Scotch(es) and our beers, without talking much while there. It seemed to me that the locals were quite keen not to engage in conversation. A couple offered condolences, but equally were much relieved by Jim's monosyllabic thanks. I wondered how many of them knew more than they would let on, or who were friends of Dickie and Marigold, as a couple. Were they awaiting her triumphant return? Were they fair weather companions, who could simply turn the page and move on? We had an early night. Not so Anne, who had now acclimatised and wanted to explore the flat and make up for time wasted dozing in the car. Rosy was not at her best in the morning.

1 Dr Grech and the Will Reading

Jim let me drive, a sure sign he was brooding, inland to Mosta. We had booked the first possible appointment with Dr Grech, but still arrived some while ahead of it, much to his amusement. I blamed unusually amiable traffic, he offered that we had not adjusted to the Maltese clock; and we both knew that nerves could not settle until we had lanced the boil of The Will. Anne kept Rosy busy. More likely, Rosy made sure Anne kept her busy. Jim was stewing quietly. Dr Grech exchanged a few routine pleasantries with me, or to be exact, he was gently probing to see what I was made of and getting a picture of how I might react. I played my part and asked a few trivial questions to keep the chat going, and ease Jim into the deeper waters slowly.

"Please excuse me, this is my first time in Malta. I am pretty ignorant, although my Father flew in and out with the RAF in, I think, 1941 to 1944. He took some lovely black and white photos of old churches and streets. 'Grech' I see is a popular and upmarket family name. What does the suffix 'Mifsud' mean?"

He laughed. "Very little. It is another of Malta's most common surnames, and my wife's maiden name. The RAF! May I thank him, through you, and all who came with him. They were difficult days. The airport was then between here and Mdina, at Ta'Qali. You should go and take Rosy and Anne: it is more of a tourist and craft centre now. Your

52

father's photos are almost certain to be at Mdina – classical church facades, and hilltop walls?" I nodded. Just that.

He turned to Jim.

"I hope the funeral went as well as these things ever can. My respects. Now, let's see what we can do to make the best of the situation." He was looking at Jim, but, I felt, really addressing me. I hurriedly started trying to make a few notes.

"Congratulations on you all getting here quickly. On reflection, that has made all the difference. If I understand your late father's lifestyle correctly, he was on the relaxed side with formalities, such as door keys. May I suggest that you change the locks, on the house and the garage this morning? Here is the address of a handyman in Bugibba. I have taken the liberty of telling him you will be calling in.

"This really is most helpful. Possession, as they say, really is nine tenths of the law and gives us, sorry, I mean you, rather better leverage."

"What's the ****** point? That ***ing gold-digger gets it all anyway!" As farmers go, Jim swore rarely. That he was now showed he had not absorbed yesterday's little teaser. Dr Grech was not put out in the slightest. "Quite so, quite so. That is indeed what Mr Richard's Last Will states. Ms Marigold is entitled to the lifetime use of all the Maltese estate: in short, that is what that strange (English!) legal word 'usufruct' generally means. If, that is, you accept the Will."

Jim was close to exploding, but a calming courtroom wave got him to bide his time. He purred on.

[Interrupting him, in type only, a little legal clarification of my own. Time has passed. I am not legally trained. Or do I mean not trained in legal fields? I report the case, but I have changed some aspects, subtly, as our conversations were subject to privilege. So, any errors you may find are deliberate. That's my excuse and I am sticking to it. Can you skip this dense, technical chapter? Certainly not! This is the key to the whole sorry story and has cost sweated blood to write. Pray continue, Dr Grech.]

"This will take a little time. Bear with me. Maltese law is mostly close to familiar British case law, but we have picked up some Continental practices from the Code Napoleonic structure. This is especially evident, and relevant, in relation to inheritance, and what happens in the absence of a…ahem…viable will."

He looked my way. I was scribbling frantically, and kept my head well down, lest he could see my complete incomprehension. Not that he needed to look to be aware of that. I did however recall that one dust-free tome on Usufruct, and it started to dawn on me just why the old genius was ticking along so smoothly. I also noticed that he had started to refer to Mr Richard in a detached, formal and bloodless way, as if his time has passed, in more than one sense. He was also very careful not to mention who was or was not present when the Will in Quo was committed to paper and sealed.

(14) Local legal papers

2 What Was Writ

"As I was instructed to write, and witness, Mr R Chalybeate's almost dying expression was that everything belonging to Mrs Agnes—whose late estate has, as is usual—been added to Mr Richard's interests, and his own would pass to you, as their eldest son. Am I right in thinking that you have a younger brother, a Mr Edward Chalybeate? And that owing to an earlier difference of opinions, or 'massive falling out' is I believe it might be phrased, your parents had already decided not to mention him in either of their wills?"

Jim nodded his agreement, under sufferance. He was close to tears, with now two painful memories re-agitated. When he asked to pop outside for a smoke, everyone was mightily relieved. Everyone, that is, except young Anne, who at the tender age of half a year, had already spotted soft spots in

Grandad Jim that the rest of us had not found in decades, and how to milk them. "Aye, you carry on with Iain here. He's a lot better at talking and writing than he is at doing, so it'll be right."

Trust me on this one, that was a compliment, gratefully accepted.

We carried on.

"As written, it is indeed correct that your father/ father-in-law, Jim, gets the whole estate, but only upon the death of Ms Marigold, who has full use of it all for the length of her days. I am not privy to the details, but she would appear to be in her late 50s, and in tolerable health, so the wait might be some decades. Worse, although she is legally bound to maintain the value of flat, car, cash, properties in Bradford, and so on, this is hard to enforce. Even harder to chase her beyond her own grave. In short, Jim might be in his own dotage, and left with only the shells of some buildings of less than investment quality."

3 A Test of Wills

"But. There is another way of looking at the problem. As I touched upon yesterday, your late grandfather's intentions (and the 'guidance' offered him) overlooked a number of aspects, notably your grandmother's own estate. I fear I may have been remiss in not pointing this out at the time, but in my own defence, the whole exercise did seem a trifle rushed and entered into with a narrow sense of purpose."

I felt I had to try and prove I was up to speed. I think I could dimly see the outlines of a silhouette of a Plan B, or even Dr Grech's own Plan A, with the actual Will being something of a red herring, and a smelly one at that. "Would I be right in thinking that your advice is to reject the will?"

Impressive, eh! As he had said exactly that the previous day, I thought I was sound here. "And from what you are suggesting, if that happens, Ms Marigold gets only Jim's possessions, but not Agnes'? I suppose half now is better than all, much eroded, much later."

"Very good, young Iain. That is a fair deduction, from what you have heard so far. But it is more complex, and rather better than that. By rejecting the Will, Jim both rules himself out of benefits, and means that Mr Richard died partially intestate: without a valid complete testament. Under Maltese law, Mrs Agnes' half does indeed pass straight to Jim, as now being her intention, and not via her surviving spouse's. But Mr Richard's own estate (half) does not allow his dependents to be ignored. Ms Marigold is named as the beneficiary, in this run of events; but Jim, now in this case HIS oldest surviving descendant gets 1/3 as of right."

Rosy was quicker on this than me. "Hang on, I am Jim's oldest child. Does that mean I get 1/3 and her ladyship from Bradford gets 2/3?"

"Well done, Rosy. Yes, but that is only of Richard's half. Together with your grandma's half, Jim and you are now— sorry, would now be if this is pursued—in charge of fully 2/3 of all assets: properties here and in Yorkshire, any monies on deposit, the car, and so on. As you are here, first, and with the keys, and in possession, you have the upper hand. Cash can be removed from the bank, And as I mentioned, the locks changed. You have had a very lucky escape.

"The day ticks on. We have covered a lot of complex ground. Against my normal rhythm, may I, in this instance, suggest you all revert to UK time, and an urgent bit of it at that, and get going? You will need a little time to reflect, and possibly to get Jim to see things from this new angle. May I dare to presume that you two, begging your pardon, Miss Anne, do you agree that this is a better outcome? Less worse, at least. Good. Farewell. Where is your first stop?"

I held up the card. "To the locksmiths! Back to the flat, and change door and garage keys, and add an anti-theft bar to the car steering wheel and clutch. Then to the bank, with the official funeral documents, so that Jim can assume power of attorney. Huge thanks, Dr Grech! We are hugely in your debt."

"Not a bit of it, Iain. Do please call me Lesley. I was very fond of Agnes, and even, until recently, Richard. I am only too happy to be of assistance; but the thanks go to the ancient and oft arcane details of the law of our little island—most of which is down to British creativity. Do enjoy your day.

"We will meet again soon. There is more to discuss. We are not quite out of the woods, yet." An odd phrase, for an almost treeless island. "While we may, with luck, have the advantage, we will still need to persuade her of this, and a settlement will have to be made. Iain, you will have to sell this to Jim."

But his parting words, uttered genially, chilled me. "I am glad you got here first. Had Ms Marigold or her allies done so, I would have been obliged to act for them. Good day."

4 Tidying Up

Despite this horrendous roll of the dice, which I opted not to relay, until now, the walled oasis of Villa Grech-Mifsud seemed even more idyllic as we floated out. The fountains more musical, the lemons especially inviting – I weakened, and 'borrowed' one, against the eventual capital from the estate – and the cool breeze energised us. Even Jim seemed more relaxed after his solitude among the figs and kiwis, and classical Graces.

We stopped for a rare midday beer, at a cool bar on the edge of Mosta, and Rosy and I went through the useful bits with Jim. Although he still smarted at the idea of a payout, he didn't take much persuading that Dr Grech's plan was a lot better than the Will had seemed only a few days ago. He was happy to let us take over and promised to sign anything when needed.

I drove back to Bugibba, but my paranoid eye rested mostly on the rear mirror, as I presumed every dark windowed limo behind us was a lynch mob, intent on removing keys, car and any number of limbs as light collateral. But the journey was bliss, by Maltese traffic standards.

(15) Locks

The locksmith was a man to trust, just as well, as we had cause to lean on him again later, and the locks were duly changed. Oddly, the garage seemed already airier, and the jerry can count seemed to have evaporated. I am sure there were more bits of Perkins outdoor motors in there yesterday. But no matter, that suited us nicely. The Wolseley slept indoors for the first time in years.

Afternoon by the seaside, a short drive round the corner at Popeye's Village: ideal for Anne, fewer prying eyes for us. Jim relaxed for the first time. I had not realised what a powerful swimmer he had been, as he sliced across the bay and back. We bought Anne a Popeye and Olive Oyl inflatable paddling pool, complete with a spinach themed bottom. She lived in it and slept much better. Therefore, so did we.

(16) Popeye's Village, Mellieha, NW Malta (SAH)

5 Relaxation, At Last

Next day, we had some more jobs to take care of, but largely were able to wind down, and hit the beach, and take Anne for a tour of the St Paul's bay in a rented rowing boat. With a picnic on board. And a parasol.

In the afternoon, I drove across to Mosta and called in on Dr Grech to confirm agreement, and run through the next steps, known and probable. It seemed highly likely that a trip across during half term in May would be needed, by which time papers should be ready.

I thanked Dr Grech profusely and made a mental note to bring him something suitable from home. Being the epitome of charm and manners, as usual, he said, "Do look me up whenever you need. Nowhere is over an hour by taxi, except for Valetta's traffic jams. Come and have a glass of my own wine – a bit better than the plonk they sell to unwitting tourists!"

The following day, Jim headed home to the farm, and Rosy and I headed back to work. At about the same time, news of Dickie's death reached Bradford, and we must follow it there.

5 Gold Digging, or Heart of Gold?

1 Work

Marigold, Nelly to all and sundry in The White Rose, was in her natural habitat. Getting the pub ready for opening is the least agreeable part of bar staff's duties. The light is poor, last night's smells have been locked in without chance of escape, the carpet is still sticky and when you do get the doors open, the first men through are usually those you least want to see.

(17) The White Rose Pub, Bradford (SAH)

Still, if she was a few minutes late getting in, the boss had not appeared, so no problem and no distraction. The postman had caught her as she was coming out of her door and was in a chatty mood. Most of her letters were bills or junk, so she re-posted them through her own letter box, and pocketed the one from Malta. The brown paper and the stamp was familiar, the writing not; not from Dickie, so she put it aside and forgot all about it. Halfway through her shift, she remembered it, but could not find a moment of quiet time to open it. Something did not feel just right; another good reason not to be rushing.

Decades of bar work behind her, she was perfectly capable of pouring drinks, totting up the bill, and appearing to chat to regulars while her mind was elsewhere. In Bugibba and Sleima, of course. Her first holiday in Malta had been a quick week's escape; a bit of sun and sea, a chance to let someone else pour her a drink for a change, preferably a daft coloured one with a silly name and a paper parasol. Anyone in the bar, sorry, cocktail lounge, would have thought she was enjoying her own party, and the life and soul of it. Superficially, that was true enough. She was well able to strike up conversations, chat away and make people laugh, including herself. But that easy familiarity had a dark side. Relationships tended not to get much further.

2 Alone

That was half frustration and sadness, and half defensive self-protection. She was wary of letting anyone get too close. Having married a bit suddenly and a bit before she was ready, she was devastated by her husband's sudden death while their daughter, Julie, was still a babe in arms. Naturally, he had left no money, no provision, and no will. Thanks to the lorry and the parapet, nothing worth salvaging from his pride and joy, his BSA, either. It had been the other, possibly even the main, love of his life, either on the road or more often in bits in the yard, being tweaked, polished or repaired. Young men are immortal, until they aren't. Carefree, and leaving the pieces—in his case all too literally—to others.

Bringing up Julie with little help, financial or affectionate, had been tough, and she was very cagey about committing herself again. True enough, she did have a man in tow, sort of, but it was all a bit on and off, a well short of marriage of convenience, to both. They would see each other for a while, and fill some gaps in each other's needs, but then drift away again.

Marigold was all too aware she had to look after herself, and look out for her now mid-teens princess, herself now well into the high-risk times. Despite the hours being long and the cash being short, she did her best to look her best and keep the inevitable ravages wrought by time at bay.

3 Adventure

Malta was a quick dream and a chance to escape for a while. It was on her second trip that she chanced into The Swordfish and ended in a corner with a bunch of lively and entertaining old men, Dickie amongst them. Their Northern English banter was all too familiar from home, and similarly, some of them were all too familiar. If at first, she was spoiled for choice, of a sort, one by one they fell away, and she found herself spending more time with Dickie.

Even so, she was surprised by his later invitation, in his own unique spidery hand, to come out again, and even more surprised that she accepted. It was a relationship of mutual convenience. She was well aware that he was only recently widowed but chose not to think through too many parts of that too deeply. She rationalised herself into saying that she was offering a happier memory of Bradford days, the more so as his own family had cooled on him. Having a special friend and a place in the sun on a part time basis was a welcome escape from dreary work routines and endless setbacks at home.

The age difference meant that this was never going to be a very long relationship, but still she convinced herself that she offered him something special, and why not enjoy a bit of credit for it, as and when her time came, meaning his went?

Snippets of this, and the up and down mixed emotions that flashed in and out of her mind, kept coming to her throughout the day's shift, which mercifully only ran until tea time. When she got home, she made a brew, and washed the pub's lingering smells and stains out, and sat down with the now slightly crumpled correspondence. She was ready for most things, she thought, but was upset and confused by what she read.

4 Dashed

The letter was from the lawyer who had helped Dickie with his Will, and she had thought him an ally. However, the key part of his over long and, she thought, rambling letter read something like this (as recalled later).

"I hope you have been informed of Mr Richard Chalybeate's recent death…"

She hadn't, and was more than a little put out that none of his, their, friends—so called—in Bugibba had bothered to tell her.

"… As you know, Mr Chalybeate mentioned you in his last will, and intended that you enjoy his estate. Unfortunately, there have been some complications, and you will be well advised to seek legal 'Advice'. I am not able to represent you in the matter, having been appointed by his surviving family to act for them. With that now formal, I cannot comment further. I would advise you to get in touch with a suitable local solicitor here. Perhaps mutual friends could suggest one; failing that, I enclose a list, with no preference, but all within a relatively short range of Bugibba."

The letter closed with all the polite formalities.

Marigold had any number of emotions. News of Dickie's death was a shock, but not a surprise. That 'friends' had not bothered was irritating and a blow to confidence. That Dickie had left her something was a welcome respite but having to fight for her fair share was depressing, three times over: she needed some good news; it was unfair that it was now a legal squabble; and she knew she had no idea how to go about it. A bad day, and she cried herself to sleep.

5 Struggle

Next day, she was on the late shift, so had the morning to get sorted. No chance of a lie in. A good strong brew and start thinking. She dug out everything she could relating to Malta: letters from Dickie, photo albums, stray receipts from meals out, even her passport to see the stamps. Anything that might produce some clues, names, phone numbers. She re-read Dr Grech's letter and studied the lawyers' list he had offered. There were two in St Paul's Bay/Bugibba. She tried phoning a Mr Spitieri first. He sounded keen, but a bit too confident.

"Yes, yes, no problem. I'll get your money back for you. Dr Grech wrote the will, you say? We'll soon see him off," she thanked him and said she would call back.

Next was a Mr Zammit. He was far less gung ho. "Tricky, tricky. You might be able to make a case. Who did you say had written the will? Lesley Grech? Oh, dear. That does not help you, I am afraid. I would be MOST surprised if he of all people has made a mistake. A complete win is out of the question. But I would guess that there is a bit of room for manoeuvre. It will be in their interests, as well as yours, to reach a settlement without troubling judges and juries. I don't want to make you any promises I can't keep, or to take the case on—and your money—if there is no chance. Leave it with me. I will make a phone call or two, off the record. Give me your number, and postal address. I will call you back by the end of the week."

His pessimism gave Marigold some relief. Better realism and a chance of a slice than breezy bogus bullshit. She unspent all the lavish dreams she had been counting, and counting on, and started thinking of a holiday with Judy after her summer exams were over. Maybe not Malta.

It was a long shift in The White Rose that afternoon/evening, but it passed quickly. The regulars didn't notice a slight change in her, but she weighed each one up, and convinced herself that her Bugibba disappointment was still preferable to any options in there. A few weeks later, she started looking for new jobs, with a more promising social mix.

Mr Zammit did call back on Friday. He seemed a little more optimistic. No, little chance of the flat – but anyway, that would be a mixed blessing and take some work and spending to get ready for sale – let the Chalybeates have that. Yes, there could be a cash pay out, not huge, but nicely into four figures. No, his charges for sorting it would not be large. Provided it did not need to go to court, it could be managed in the low three figures. Slightly wistfully, Mr Zammit noted that in Malta, lawyers don't get even a glimpse of what is charged in London. That is doubtless why the greedier of them, sorry, I mean aspirational and dynamic, try to trade Valetta for EC1. He very kindly offered to dig out and send over the copy of *The Times of Malta* with Dickie's death notice in it.

Marigold was in at least four minds: sad, grateful, frustrated, and angry. Rationally, she would take Mr Zammit's offer of help, not count any chickens, but take what she could reasonably get. Any capital sum would in truth be more use than the—what was it?—'useful fact'. She was now annoyed at the lack of help or even communication from Bugibba; and irritated that Dickie's family had got the better of her. But she decided to be a bit of a nuisance, and made a couple of phone calls, to Dickie's less law-abiding so-called business associates. Not a lot to lose, and a spot of revenge could be a bit of a laugh. She enjoyed writing a short letter to Mr Spitieri, thanking him for his encouragement, and promising to use his services throughout her next (haha) round of legal business in Malta, but sadly, not this one. She promised to pass his name on to any friends who had money they wanted rid of. Then, a more sensible letter to Mr Zammit, agreeing to his looking after her affairs, and adding a few points which might help, or at least muddy the waters, to advantage.

After that, she took Julie to the doctor's. Nothing newsworthy, least of all the appointments running to time. Marigold was flipping idly through the old and curly edged magazines, when a page of useless adverts at the back caught her eye, and gave her a malicious, but amusing idea. She slipped a couple of the magazines, which would not be missed, into her shopping bag, and bought a few stamps on the way home. A good investment.

She slept better that night, made a point of talking to Julie about her studies and social life, and suggesting they had a nice holiday after exams. No promises, but as Julie was doing Geography, she could do a spot of research as to where she'd like to go. She was much perkier on her shift, the more so when Julie popped in after school—a rare occurrence—with a few ideas, not just about holidays.

She was glad that the regulars in The White Rose all knew her as Nellie, not her real name. Marigold she might be, but she looked like missing both the marrying and the gold.

6 A Spring Migration Flight

The spring rattled past, and work routines were interrupted by Maltese correspondence, papers to check and sign, and even a rather crackly brief phone call with Dr Grech. Eventually, Rosy, Anne and I went back for a short week's visit, with a little formal business to sort out, and to make a start at sorting the flat.

1 Malta from the Air

The flight was not too crowded, and I could do a little homework, and also enjoyed the window seat, so Rosy and Anne could potter about. Paul Theroux, the great traveller, is always insistent that the thinking traveller (a superior species to lesser breeds, tourists and trippers) enjoy the novelty of the patchwork quilt of fields and villages as the plane comes into land, and speculate on the lives, hardships and dreams of the locals.

A Therouxian landscape, and cliché peoples. Nice work if you can get it. I had no such luck. I knew pretty much who we were going to meet and with the exception of the estimable Dr Grech, I wasn't looking forward to much of the diary.

We landed on runway 'Luqa 31'. Why '31'? Aircraft are much better taking off and landing into wind, a 'lift' bonus. Most airstrips face the prevailing wind, and are labelled with the compass direction, /10: so, in Malta, the common wind is from the NW, 310^0. Locally, they call it the 'Majjistal'. If the wind shifts, the same runway is used the other way, so this time 'runway 13', 130^0, SE, for the 'Xlokk' wind, known in most of the Med as the Khamseen.

Maserati named a fast car after it. Fascinating stuff, no? No, I thought not. Luqa is not interesting in the slightest. We were itching to get to its predecessor at Ta'Qali, for different reasons: me to try and wake up some ghosts from my dad's several stays there in war time; Rosy to explore the flourishing art and craft colony now in the old corrugated half cylindrical Nissen huts. It is just between Mdina and Mosta, both places on our list of essentials, for work or tourism. But that would have to wait until later in the week.

2 Gifts for the Wise Man?

Finding a suitable thank you gift for our lawyer had exercised us all for a while. What to give to someone who clearly has life sorted out and whose house and bonsai Eden are filled with glories beyond my budget, and culture. No worthy book on history, music, gardening would add to his encyclopaedic knowledge. I thought about some John Mortimer, but that would be crass. Souvenirs of Blighty? Insulting. A lavish guide to The British Museum? His house had more than enough quality exhibits, and anyway, glorying in what Empire had purloined from then supplicant colonies requires some delicate diplomacy. We hedged our bets and settled on one of Rosy's pen and ink pictures of Lake District cottage housing, and two decent bottles of French wine, a Vacqueras and a Pomerol, with Hugh Johnson's blessing. They were of course graciously received and appreciated to a wholly inscrutable degree.

3 In and About

'Sorrento', Dickie and Agnes' flat, and now half Jim's, one sixth Rosy's and theoretically one third the mystical blond Bradford barmaid's, was as we left it. Each place has its own odour, signature smell, but open windows and once round with sweeper and duster, a few scented candles and a quickly rustled up curry dispersed the echoes. Anne's paddling pool was intact, and swiftly filled with water and her; and continually emptied, splash by splash, to her giggles and gurgles.

The garage clearly had had some visitors, and our friendly neighbourhood locksmith was hastily commissioned, again. But, again, the more of the garage's contents 'liberated' by Dickie's fair-weather friends, the less we were lumbered with. He guided us to a general DIY shop, little larger than a kiosk, but stacked to the ceiling with enough variety of tools and materials. We invested in the basics, and plenty of white and pastel paints, and readied the flat for a bit of freshening up.

After the essentials, managed to explore a few of the proper tourist sights. First off, we tried using the bus, and avoiding driving. But while at the bus stop, we were kidnapped in a white Austin 1100.

(18) An Austin 1100/1300

The genuine article, with a gentle list to the left, caused by an under-serviced 'hydrolastic' suspension. Our driver was extremely keen to offer us a free cold drink and a free morning in the hotel pool. All he wanted was an hour of our time. To be exact, he needed our names on his press gang quota list, while the Time Share sales team extolled the joys of committing ourselves for life, or longer, in their resort.

Granted, after Rosy prodded Anne a couple of times, they were excused and headed for the pool, while I did my sums. Fabulous value, and an amazing opportunity. I could only see 37 things wrong with the offer, but I had only voiced three of them when I was released to the pool. We went home by bus, as the promised return taxi curiously never materialised. Back in Bugibba and St Paul's Bay, Rosy had a few calls to make, starting with her grandma's old doctor, who was suitably pleased to see her. We dined in The Swordfish, but only on the quieter evenings, and always with half a paranoid eye and ear for who might be observing us with malicious or commercial intent. Of international bodyguards there was no trace, wounded, healed, working or whatever else.

4 History in the Present

We combined our necessary trip to see Dr Grech with a spot of sightseeing in Mosta, Mdina and Ta'Qali. Mosta's dome is justly famous, and not only because of the large wartime bomb that pierced the roof but failed to explode; hailed as a modern-day miracle. But the surrounding maze of ordinary streets, corner shops and local churches are a delight, for anyone not in a hurry, or with a camera. Given the sharp light and crisp shadow, modern photography is easy.

(19) War time photos – RAF Composite; Rabat Church from the airmen's billet

Up the hill, walled Mdina is even more picturesque, and redolent of history, ancient modern, peaceful and war time. During the great siege of 1565, Mdina held out while Valetta was being battered. In 1941, stranded aircrew were billeted in the town. I was there to try and place my father's photos, taken with much more basic equipment, and a light meter. It was fairly easy, and inordinately evocative. I was glad I have never had to be in uniform.

(20) Mdina, December 1942, from Ta'Qali

Ta'Qali held no ghosts, flying or ground crew. The runway has gone, or rather had been reduced to a concrete archipelago of foundations and parking areas. The barracks and workshops have had their brick ends repainted in bright colours and were now home to a thriving mix of artists and craft sellers and makers. Rosy was in her element and furnished Anne with colourful diversions, the flat with pictures and ceramic decorations, and her suitcase with beads for the natives back home.

Our next excursion was less successful. Mea culpa. We drive to see some of the very many ancient stone relics. The ground on the limestone plateau looked dry enough. But the Wolseley is certainly not built for off roading, not least as its tyres were barely fit for dry tarmac, let alone sliding mud. We had to be rescued. The ruins remained unvisited.

(21) Ta'Qali, old airfield, newer craft village (SAH)

5 Viticulture

Never ones to shy away from enormous personal risk, we then tried a local wine tasting. Malta being small and dry, local grape production is severely limited, and most wine is made from 'must' imported from Italy, Spain or even N Africa. Most is table wine quality, at best, but local producers are trying hard to get respectable quality.

Wine tourism is in its infancy. We managed to get a few samplings, of the distinctive Ġellewża (red) and Girgentina (white) produce. Marsovin is the largest and have been around since 1907, but Camilleri, Montekristo and Meridiana, are also worth looking up, not least for their cellar tours. Having whetted your taste buds, no point in pre-empting your own enjoyable sippings and quaffings.

6 Legal Culture

For us, saying wine in Malta means Dr Grech, and midweek, we were summoned for a spot of business, and also a glass or two of his own, very excellent and individual home brew. He even had some homemade orange juice and dried figs for Anne. He gave us an update on progress. The testatee had engaged a sensible lawyer, who was sure to look for a beneficial pay out for her, playing on the obvious situation that endless dispute and delay was not in the Chalybeates' interests. Nonetheless, the outlines of a deal were in sight. Jim would not be best pleased, but he smiled warmly at me, to say, that's my job. Banking matters and cash were solvable;

Agnes' properties in Bradford can probably be kept out of the equation, and the Wolseley was not an asset worth fighting for.

He did not know quite how right he was, as he smiled broadly at Rosy, not me. I can only assume he had read my simple mind and sought to spare her from my nascent collecting instinct, which ignored shipping, storage, repair, spare parts and rust related ill-judged dreams. Some 24 mpg is tolerable on an island as small as Malta: silly as anything but a show car in GB.

"That leaves 'Sorrento', Mr and Mrs Chalybeate's, and now, de facto and mostly de jure, your property. What will you do with it?"

Rosy was ready. "Much as we'd like to keep it, let our assorted families use it, and maintain a toe hold connection to Malta, there is not the collective appetite for it. Farmers get few enough weeks off, and they have little to gain from being tied to one spot. I will come back, to see Grandma Agnes' grave, but on balance, we expect to return in the summer, try and freshen the place up, then put it on the market."

Dr Grech refreshed my glass, despite knowing full well I was driving. "All too sensible. Prices are not too bad at the moment, and the exchange rate favours you as capital exporters, not you as tourists. You might think of getting the locksmith to add extra locks on the main doors. Don't work too hard on the flat – a lick of paint won't add much to its real value – better enjoy as much of St Paul's Bay while you are here—this is your holiday!"

We had done as much as we could, and work beckoned. An extra lock was added to the flat, but not the garage. We said farewell to the flat, looking forward to an easy and cheap summer holiday; and said goodbye to the Wolseley, though we did not know that at the time.

As the plane left Luqa and started climbing, I spotted the outlines of Ta'Qali and Mdina on its hilltop, then as a bonus, St Paul's Bay, but otherwise, did not look down, or back. Exactly where the predictably unexpected thrills and spills were queuing up, out of view, in the patchwork quilt of small streets of Bugibba and St Pauls, soon out of sight and mind, for a while.

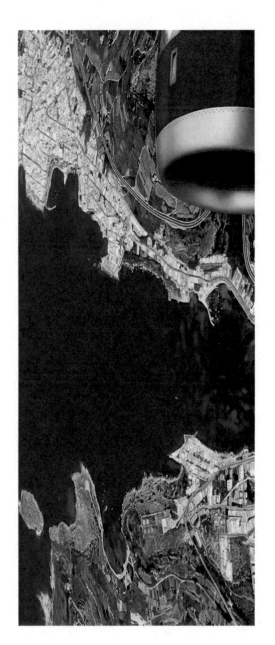

(22) Parting thoughts over Bugibba & St Paul's Bay

7 A Hot Cross Maltese

1 Once More unto the Beach

The end of the school year is always hectic and does not allow much time for diversions. I was dimly aware that Jim had heard from Dr Grech but did not ask for details. We booked a fortnight's holiday in late July and hoped that with Anne now being a few months older and almost walking, she would cope in the heat. A bit of good news, Rosy invited her old PE colleague Gail to come and join is for one of the weeks, and gaily offered to pick her up in the trusty Wolseley.

The weather did not disappoint, or help, depending on point of view. It was blistering. We got to the flat in the late heat of the afternoon, and all three of us had a rapid cold shower, then we inflated and half-filled Anne's favourite Popeye pool, which kept her happy. We had about survived the journey, and enjoyed the sunset, through duty free filled glasses. At a respectable hour, we walked town to the quay and dined at The Swordfish. But on the way home, I stayed at quay level and had a look at the garage. The simple lock had been forced, and the Wolseley was missing, along with what else was left of any possible value. Still, plenty of junk to dump, mind. Claiming our inheritance threw up a few little snags, of which this was the first.

We hired a car and collected Gail in due course. She was amused and not at all sorry to miss her promised chauffer driven ride in Dickie's venerable limo but was concerned by the circumstances. She was a great asset, adding numbers to our patrols, decorating while Rosy looked after Anne, or vice versa, and offering a fresh and impartial point of view when we hit snags and decision points.

She still had plenty of time to show off her swimming strengths, and occasionally her water skiing, and she did her Christmas shopping early at Ta'Qali. She and Rosy bought enough things, decorative and practical, to give the flat a fresh feel. With the former housemates in retail harmony, my opinion was not sought, or if offered, considered.

2 Car Wars, or Wars, or War

Locating the car was surprisingly easy, which was a worry. Nobody knew anything about it, not a thing. But any number of 'helpful' souls suggested exactly where I might look, almost to the house number, and practically queued up for tickets to the spectacle. They were unanimous as to the name, even, a Mr Farrugia.

(23) A Wolseley 16/60. Not Mr Chalybeate's

Like all great generals, if I could not choose the terrain (away fixture), I could choose the hour – early in the cool of the morning, just after those who go to work had gone. I armed myself with photocopies of the key documents, climbed the two steps to door floor height, knocked on the door, stepped back down and readied my battle speech. My putative duellist arrived promptly and accepted the challenge. You might expect me to say he was not best pleased to see me. But he seemed happy to have the encounter. He almost smiled as he looked down on me, arms folded. Tall, very tall by Maltese standards, and with the kind of build that comes from lifting fishing nets and parts of boats, lifting cars (he had clearly lifted 'our' car) and heavy wheelbarrows and hods, not any namby pamby mirrored exercises in gyms. His nose had seen combat. His sleeveless vest the same. His arms were folded, revealing the ample room for the ample tattoos which adorned them. As kinetic art, they spoke to me of naval history, and of having been paid for on Straight Street in Valetta. Any retired British naval rating will happily rate the pleasures of Straight Street to you.

His half smile altered little on hearing my opening salvo of 'I have come to collect my car', but as I said it, all my saliva deserted me, and robbed me of the dramatic punch line. Mr Farrugia kindly filled in with his own punch line, which went, as I recall, something like:

"This is MY car. Dickie and Marigold gave it to me. I have the car, I have the keys, and you can shove your paperwork anywhere you like. I'll help. If you don't remove your pointing arm NOW, I will show you my origami skills using your bones, if there are any in there."

I had no desire to resemble a failed Libyan bodyguard, which even then was a so last year look, so I conceded that point. Unfortunately, he anticipated my next move.

"And don't waste my—or your—time talking about the law. My cousin is a lawyer, he lives round the corner, Mr Spitieri. Marigold has already contacted him. My brother is PC Farrugia – that's his house just up the road. From the look of the windows, he will be off to work any moment, and if you are still here, you will nicely make his first arrest of the day, after he has called the ambulance. Before you mention it, no, it wasn't me who broke into the garage to 'liberate' MY car, and I have a dozen witnesses who didn't see me do it. Now, Bugibba off."

You will agree with me that there are obviously a number of legal and moral flaws in his reasoning and evidence. I felt I had won the technical side of the debate. However, I did not want to humiliate him, and with a stinging 'You have not heard the last of this!', I turned with surprising dignity and left the scene. Mr Farrugia waved me off with a short Maltese salutation, which I could not find in my phrase book.

On reflection, a modern hire car has lots of advantages, from mpg to working suspension by way of reduced risk, and I concluded I was lucky to have got rid of the Wolseley. My good friend Mr Farrugia could sort out all the problems, and good luck to him. 'We' did start 'our' classic car collection, with a much racier and more eye-turning model, still from the Austin-Morris-Riley-Wolseley-Standard-MG-Triumph-Rover-Jaguar-BLMC-BL stable, but that is another story, from eight years later.

I walked back to the flat. Rosy was pleased to see me; Gail was much amused. There are winners and losers. Possession really is 9/10 of the law. Tattoos are effective as war paint. I won, due to lessons learned.

3 A Chill Summer

Despite the heat, the rest of the trip and holiday had a cold, clammy feel about it. There was more lock changing, some redecorating, a bit of sightseeing, and plenty of beach activity. We didn't rush to The Swordfish, it now being very clear we were at the prey end of any harpoons, not the hunter end.

That said, we did venture in one evening when they advertised live football: England v Italy. It may have been billed as a friendly, I forget the circumstances, but there is no such thing for a Maltese audience. Football is second only to politics as a way of getting local emotions to boiling point. Lacking a competitive national team of their own, despite passionate best efforts, 'bigger' matches act as surrogates.

(24) Straight Street, Valetta. Without sailors or others (LMA)

Politics in Malta (this is leading straight back to football, promise) is a rowdy affair. Elections are hard, and noisily fought. A 51-49 result is seen as a landslide. The pro-independence movement started in the 1920s, but the Union Jack (yes, that, being on RN ships) did not finally go until the late 1970s. Football as with independence, the pro-and anti-English factions were evenly split, so a football game is the ideal chance for a bit of tribal loyalty and letting off steam. You can guess most of the split. The expat English (let's leave those of Scots, Welsh or Irish origin for another time) are more True Brit than actual Brits are; the nationalists and those with Maghrebian tendencies will shout for anyone else.

If you want to be truly brave, pop into a Malta bar and start a discussion about politics; or shout for the wrong team without checking the bar's colours in advance. Or, have a heavy evening on Maltese wine. Then again, if you do all three together, you might just get lucky! The passion for politics and football won't have dimmed; but in combination, there might be enough confusion for you to survive.

In truth, I don't remember the match. We kept our colours to ourselves and watched the frenetic action—in the bar, the match was dull—with careful detachment. I didn't spot my friend Mr Farrugia, either of them.

We tidied up the flat, to a presentable sellable state, removed all family heirlooms (mostly the surviving remnants of ancestral porcelain sets), and put it on the market. A final, sadly, pleasant chat with Dr Grech, and away we went. There were plenty of details to resolve, none of which needed us there in person. But there is something of Malta that has got stuck in the psyche.

(25) Rosy's photo of Mdina Church

Five Houses in Search of a Plot

Summer over, back to work and back home. Although living some distance away, we kept in more than usual touch with Jim and the farm, and with Malta. 'Sorrento' sold reasonably quickly, and at not a bad price, helped by the ever-sinking Pound, and we waited for settlement.

1 Symbolic Castles

Owning property is a peculiarly English obsession. Nowhere in the world, Celtic North and West Britain included, and most certainly Europe across the Channel has or aspires to the levels of home ownership as we do. The phrase 'An Englishman's home is his castle' is more accurate and precise than most one-line aphorisms. With that of course, we obsess about house prices more than we do about the weather. We plunge into absurd debt so as to be 'owners', at the mercy of not at all partners banks. We over inflate prices, and then wonder why the job market is so sticky.

As we have seen in Mosta, most of the world is happy to hide whatever wealth is in their pied a terre, behind as drab an exterior as is possible. Not so chez Albion. Two astute Anglophile Italians express the world's confusion best; 'Despite your weather, English homes are very strange – the house is full of plants, and the garden is full of furniture!', and, again 'When an Italian gets some money, we wear it down the street; when you English get money, you plant it in the garden.'

The Chalybeates (and me) are no exception. Much of this story was, from the beginning, rooted in property acquisitions, and the last parts of the tale concern mostly disposals.

For this purpose, the family had a bit of a family get together, general conflab and sort out. Before we join them, in the farm kitchen, of course, a few distractions and loose ends deserve a mention.

2 Property Previous

In the course of just two generous generations, the Chalybeates' various rolls of the dice have seen them land on and buy properties (green and red, and in one case, red light) in Baildon, Bradford, Morecambe, rural Lancashire, Knaresborough, and Malta. Two commercial properties, two working farms, one flat, and a handful of houses for investment. Add another generation or two of the family tree, and add in an assortment of additional houses, flats, half a chalet, and a former farmhouse, the last named more of a 'dacha' not a working producer.

As genetic curiosities go, Agnes and Richard Chalybeate had an ice cream shop and two littoral properties, one by the Med. Among their great grandchildren's residences and businesses include…an ice cream parlour, and a flat overlooking the Med. Make of that what you will.

3 Pestilential Post

Grace, Rosy's Mum, was never one to complain, but she did comment that they had received a torrent of junk mail over the summer, all addressed to the Chalybeates, all at the farm's right address, bar one small mistake in the postcode. That rang a small bell, and I looked through some of the early Malta legal correspondence, and found the same error there, later corrected.

The post was mountainous and contained everything you could possibly order by post: mail order catalogues galore, clothing for the fuller figure, classic books in impossible sets, all bound in luxurious simulated leatherette, coach holiday brochures, cures for piles, snoring, insomnia, corns, yellowing teeth, and greying hair. There were garden seed samples, stairlift special offers, double glazing upgrades, loft insulation sponsorships, and grow your own encyclopaedia sets, which would take only a few decades to complete. In short, a blasted nuisance, (other b-adjectives are available), and vast amounts of time and phone calls and stamps wasted trying to stem the flow. I don't recall one single once in a lifetime unbeatable offer being accepted.

4 Past and Possible Payouts

After the several inevitable rounds of light legal sparring, a payout was agreed, reluctantly on both sides, and duly settled up. We were at the farm for a family round table. Jim was grumbling, but no more than routinely so. "So that's the end of our Malta period. 'Sorrento' has gone, and from that, her ladyship paid off. Thanks to Rosy for fettling it to help the sale. Iain here managed to lose the car, fool. Rosy and Anne have had a couple of decent holidays in the sun. That only leaves Mum's (Grandma Agnes' to most of you) houses in Bradford."

"I am not getting any younger and need to think about our Wills, and what to do with the Farm, when Grace's and my days are done. Rosy, I always promised you a third, of what the farm was, before your brothers started working on it, and we had to expand it. Would you like the proceeds from Malta instead?"

Rosy managed not to cry, and ever so politely declined the offer. "We are just about breaking even now, despite me not working while Anne was little. Use the money to clear some of the farm's loans, Dad, which will be more valuable and useful."

"Thanks, Rosy. Good Girl." He didn't manage to prevent a moist eye. "I won't forget." He did.

5 Asset Stripping?

The Bradford houses discussion followed similar lines. Rosy again declined to take on responsibility, or the dubious capital therein. They were not brilliant investments, as either rental income or capital growth. When each became vacant, they got sold, each paying for a small field or so. Those that stayed rented consumed more time and effort than was worthwhile.

Jim was forever having to press for late rent, or send Rosy's brother, generally known as Sid (long before British Gas borrowed his name) across to fix a leak here, a broken toilet there, replace guttering or do a bit of handyman work for inept tenants. He was especially enthusiastic about getting rid.

That evening, in the pub, Sid confided in Rosy and me just why. For us, it was sufficient reason that he preferred looking after his own cows, or building/repairing/welding assets that helped the farm, to say nothing of useless travel time to and from Bradford. But after a couple of Guinnesses, he told us another very good reason. He had only recently been across to one of the houses, somewhere like Crossgate Street, so I am told, that needed work doing, for a tenant who was behind with her rent. She had an uncertain income, from a profession that did not involve regular hours, but could mean gainful employment at any time of day, evening or night. While he was fixing whatever it was, she made a kind offer to reward him in kind, avoiding any complicated cash issues.

I have no doubt the offer was meant in good faith, but most unusually for Sid, he rushed to finish, and did a Le Mans start to his pickup and was lucky not to get a speeding ticket as he fled the vice rife city. I am confident he has not been to or near Bradford since.

(26) Houses on Crossgate St, Bradford (SAH)

I think that was the last house to be sold, ending the Thwaites' and Chalybeates' couple of centuries' relationship with Bradford.

6 Tempus Fugit

Farms are different, and with them the houses that yeoman farmers and their families need on site. As for the rest, time moves on. The Chalybeate seniors' property portfolio has now all gone; but younger generations have striven to get their own small, usually terraced or Nth floor, castles wherever their work and careers have taken them. Permanence is ephemeral.

9   Reckoning Up

We are almost done, but not quite. There are a few loose ends and matters that invite pause for thought. I know little more about Marigold and Julie. Their share of the 'Sorrento' sale (etc) was not life changing, but a useful sum.

It would be impolite of me, not to say crass, to divulge actual figures. Whether Marigold is still at The White Rose, or whether she has found a companion is not for this tale to relate. She does appear to have stopped collecting magazines from waiting rooms. Mr Farrugia and our Wolseley may still be roaming the mean streets of Bugibba. One day, Rosy and I hope to revisit Malta. We will keep our eyes open, and report back. I don't intend making another effort at retrieval.

On the occasion of his 80th birthday, Dr Grech hung up his last briefs, so to say, and retired to his Edenic garden. He wrote a lovely letter to Jim and me, which I still have and treasure, to say that he was tidying up his office, and would it be safe to get rid of all old cases and their papers. Sadly, there are no known 'before and after' photos of his office.

1 To Malta, If You Will

What of Malta? At the time of the Chalybeates' move there, Malta was in one of its periodic times of turmoil. The

British state had drawn in its claws, and purse strings. With the British Pound declining, Brits in Bermuda shorts were not numerous enough to replace those in naval attire. A noisy time of nationalism followed, before the three islands rethought their future.

Despite the loss of 'The Old Grey Funnel Line's' warships to work on, commercial ship repair partially filled the gap. The now independent islanders were far too canny to fall for overtures with ulterior motives from Libya, and careful strategic non-alignment has been maintained. Malta joined the EU in 2004 and swapped the Maltese Lira for the Euro in 2008. EU membership has confirmed Malta's success and maturing democracy. Tourism has rebounded, and all sorts of other industries have benefited from being part of the EU's large single market. Education is key to much success, directly and indirectly. The universities are increasingly popular on the international market. Notably, they offer medical training at a fraction of the cost of northern Europe, let alone USA.

Does Malta, GC beckon? Are you itching to join the next set of (peaceful) invaders. Modern Malta is thriving. Not without challenges, but it is a safe place for a holiday, and a good place to live. What Malta is no longer is a British museum or left-over gem of a time warp. Those days have passed. A chapter closed, clearly past its sell by date. It is a moot point which country has done better since. Who has the better future?

(27)

2 Strife After Death

At the personal level, this unexpected adventure offered lessons for all of us. As the old saying has it, all too accurately, 'Where There's a Will, There's a Relative'. Life is much simpler when you don't fall out with family. When smoothly. It being a farm, it took an inordinate length of time and far too many visits to idle solicitors. There were many times when we all wished for Dr Grech's expertise, not to mention his bills.

There is no such thing as a simple Will, if more families are involved. Uncle Ed was to prove this, after his own passing, some decades later. That, however, must wait for the sequel, or for the quel if this piece is a prequel.

3 Proper Tea Reflections

We were back at the farm for Christmas, not long after these events came to their conclusion. As often happens, there was a wholly unplanned family round table, with a decent pot of tea for all, when the subject of Malta popped up. Jim was unusually gracious in thanking Rosy and me for our time and efforts getting it sorted, with only a seasonal pantomime coda to the effect that of course, I could have done it better, to keep up appearances, and with a broad smile.

Sid has a clear evidence base regarding my inability to pick up farming skills or knowledge. So, he could not resist asking what I might have learned from the challenges.

"If I may, most of this started when Granddad was a mounted policeman in Bradford, then Jim was exercising horses on Morecambe beach; then starting a farm with a horse. We are the wrong end of the Med for 'beware of Greeks bearing gifts'. But there have been a lot of offers that have needed refusing; The will; settling for the car; Brother's efforts at collecting the rent in kind, in Bradford. Rosy offered the Malta flat, and/or the remaining Bradford houses, with occupants, instead of her share of the will.

"All thanks but no thanks. Moral of all of these stories: Always look a gift horse in the mouth."

"Not bad," conceded Jim. "We'll maybe make a farmer out of you yet."

"I told you, Jim, that lad is not as daft as he looks." Thanks, Grace.

For myself, there were quite a few other thoughts, which I opted not to lay bare in public.

As this all started, I was already behind with the in-tray wrestling. Note to me: be better ahead of self in case of the all too frequent unforeseen extra challenges. Again. Have I managed that? Read the next thrilling instalment of this saga to find out, or not.

Living and working abroad is addictive, and generally very rewarding, in one sense or another. What is essential is exploring the local psyche. Getting to know the culture and way of thinking is vital. 'Common sense' and 'the obvious' are really very local quirks, of little value outside of the domestic comfort zone.

Making the effort to get by, at least, in the local language is essential, even in places where the locals speak English better than we do. It is a worrying thought that the UK and the USA both stand out as the world's worst learners of other people's languages (not to mention plenty of lacunae with mastering our own). In an epoch when both countries are retreating into xenophobic isolationism, this must be a contributory factor. The UK recently came a clear bottom in take up of modern foreign languages at school, and rates have plummeted in the handful of years since. Not good omens for 'Global Britain'. Note to me: keep travelling, keep working on my own competences.

Living abroad is great. But it can be a fossilisation – desiccated old fruit withering on the vine; or a souring time warp – self-exiled immigrants clinging vainly and impotently to imperial echoes of faded glories.

There is an all too poplar saying in the prevalent zeitgeist of 'live in the moment', and not be concerned with past or future. Sod that. A counsel of laziness, naïve hedonism and inability to cope with the inevitable unexpected.

No, be ready for what the fates have for you round the corner.

Fittingly, Dr Grech gets the last words. Like everything in the Mediterranean, and other regions, he had a friend of a cousin (or was it the cousin of a friend?) who worked where it mattered. As the Russians say, "Never buy anything 'off the street', always check with a friend of a friend first."

Time may or may not be absolute. What we make of it is up to us. There is Maltese Time and there is British Time. Both have their place. Know when which is the more useful.

(28) Timed out

The End. Unless a sequel appears.